Blue Moose
and
Return
of the
Moose

• • • • • • • • • •

written and illustrated by
DANIEL
MANUS
PINKWATER

BULLSEYE BOOKS • RANDOM HOUSE • NEW YORK

A BULLSEYE BOOK PUBLISHED BY RANDOM HOUSE, INC.
Copyright © 1975, 1979 by Manus Pinkwater
Cover art copyright © 1993 by Steve Björkman

Library of Congress Catalog Card Number: 93-22614
ISBN: 0-679-84717-0
RL: 5.2
First Bullseye Books edition: October 1993

Manufactured in the United States of America
10 9 8 7 6 5 4 3 2

New York, Toronto, London, Sydney, Auckland

Blue Moose

for Otsu

The moose shines bright,
The stars give a light,
And you may kiss a porcupine
At ten o'clock at night.

The moose is blue,
Your wish will come true.

Moose meeting

Mr. Breton had a little restaurant on the edge of the big woods. There was nothing north of Mr. Breton's house except nothing, with trees in between. When winter came, the north wind blew through the trees and froze everything solid. Then it would snow. Mr. Breton didn't like it.

Mr. Breton was a very good cook. Every day, people from the town came to his restaurant. They ate gallons of his special clam chowder. They ate plates of his special beef stew. They ate fish stew and Mr. Breton's special homemade bread. The people from the town never talked much and they never said anything about his cooking.

"Did you like your clam chowder?" Mr. Breton would ask.

"Yup," the people from the town would say.

Mr. Breton wished they would say, "Delicious!" or, "Good chowder, Breton!" All they ever said was, "Yup." In winter they came on skis and snowshoes.

Every morning Mr. Breton went out behind his house to get firewood. He wore three sweaters, a scarf, galoshes, a woolen hat, a big checkered coat, and mittens. He still felt cold. Sometimes animals came out of the woods to watch Mr. Breton. Raccoons and rabbits came. The cold didn't bother them. It bothered Mr. Breton even more when they watched him.

One morning there was a moose in Mr. Breton's yard. It was a blue moose. When Mr. Breton went out his back door, the moose was there, looking at him. After a while, Mr. Breton went back in, closed the door, and made a pot of coffee while he waited for the moose to go away. It didn't go away; it just stood in Mr. Breton's yard, looking at his back door. Mr. Breton drank a cup of coffee. The moose stood in the yard. Mr. Breton opened the door again. "Shoo! Go away!" he said.

"Do you mind if I come in and get warm?" the moose said. "I'm just about frozen." The moose brushed past him and walked into the kitchen. His antlers almost touched the ceiling.

The moose sat down on the floor next to Mr. Breton's stove. He closed his eyes and sat leaning toward the stove for a long time. Mr. Breton stood in the kitchen, looking at the moose. The moose didn't move. Wisps of steam began to rise from his blue fur. After a long time the moose sighed. It sounded like a foghorn.

"Can I get you a cup of coffee?" Mr. Breton asked the moose. "Or some clam chowder?"

"Clam chowder," said the moose.

Mr. Breton filled a bowl with creamy clam chowder and set it on the floor. The moose dipped his big nose into the bowl and snuffled up the chowder. He made a sort of slurping, whistling noise.

"Sir," the moose said, "this is wonderful clam chowder."

Mr. Breton blushed a very deep red. "Do you really mean that?"

"Sir," the moose said, "I have eaten some very good

chowder in my time, and yours is the very best."

"Oh my," said Mr. Breton, blushing even redder. "Oh my. Would you like some more?"

"Yes, with crackers," said the moose.

The moose ate seventeen bowls of chowder with crackers. Then he had twelve pieces of hot gingerbread and forty-eight cups of coffee. While the moose slurped and whistled, Mr. Breton sat in a chair. Every now and then he said to himself, "Oh my. The best he's ever eaten. Oh my."

Later, when some people from the town came to Mr. Breton's house, the moose met them at the door. "How many in your party, please?" the moose asked. "I have a table for you; please follow me."

The people from the town were surprised to see the moose. They felt like running away, but they were too surprised. The moose led them to a table, brought them menus, looked at each person, snorted, and clumped into the kitchen.

"There are some people outside; I'll take care of them," he told Mr. Breton.

The people were whispering to one another about the moose, when he clumped back to the table.

"Are you ready to order?"

"Yup," the people from the town said. They waited for the moose to ask them if they would like some chowder, the way Mr. Breton always did. But the moose just stared at them as though they were very foolish. The people felt uncomfortable. "We'll have the clam chowder."

"Chaudière de Clam; very good," the moose said. "Do you desire crackers or homemade bread?"

"We will have crackers," said the people from the town.

"I suggest you have the bread; it is hot," said the moose.

"We will have bread," said the people from the town.

"And for dessert," said the moose, "will you have fresh gingerbread or Apple Jacquette?"

"What do you recommend?" asked the people from the town.

"After the Chaudière de Clam, the gingerbread is best."

"Thank you," said the people from the town.

"It is my pleasure to serve you," said the moose. The moose brought bowls of chowder balanced on his antlers.

At the end of the meal, the moose clumped to the table. "Has everything been to your satisfaction?" he asked.

"Yup," said the people from the town, their mouths full of gingerbread.

"I beg your pardon?" said the moose. "What did you say?"

"It was very good," said the people from the town. "It was the best we've ever eaten."

"I will tell the chef," said the moose.

The moose clumped into the kitchen and told Mr. Breton that the people from the town had said that the food was the best they had ever eaten. Mr. Breton rushed out of the kitchen and out of the house. The people from the town were sitting on the porch, putting on their snowshoes.

"Did you tell the moose that my clam chowder was the best you've ever eaten?" Mr. Breton asked.

"Yup," said the people from the town, "we said that. We think that you are the best cook in the world; we have always thought so."

"Always?" asked Mr. Breton.

"Of course," the people from the town said. "Why do you think we walk seven miles on snowshoes just to eat here?"

The people from the town walked away on their snowshoes. Mr. Breton sat on the edge of the porch and thought it over. When the moose came out to see why Mr. Breton was sitting outside without his coat on, Mr. Breton said, "Do you know, those people think I am the best cook in the whole world?"

"Of course they do," the moose said. "Do you want me to go into town to get some crackers? We seem to have run out."

"Yes," said Mr. Breton, "and get some asparagus too. I'm going to cook something special tomorrow."

"By the way," said the moose, "aren't you cold out here?"

"No, I'm not the least bit cold," Mr. Breton said. "This is turning out to be a very mild winter."

Game Warden

• • • • • • • • • • • • • • •

THERE WAS a lot of talk in town about the moose at Mr. Breton's restaurant. Some people who had never been there before went to the restaurant just to see the moose. There was an article in the newspaper about the moose, and how he talked to the customers, and brought them their bowls of clam chowder, and helped Mr. Breton in the kitchen.

Some people from other towns drove a long way with chains on their tires to Mr. Breton's restaurant, just to see the moose. Mr. Breton was always very busy waiting on tables at lunchtime and suppertime.

The moose was always very polite to the people, but

he made them feel a little uncomfortable too. He looked at people with only one eye at a time, and he was better than most of them at pronouncing French words. He knew what kind of wine to drink with clam chowder, and he knew which kind of wine to drink with the special beef stew. Some of the people in the town bragged that the moose was a friend of theirs, and always gave them a table right away. When they came to the restaurant they would pat the moose on the back, and say, "Hello, Moose, you remember me, don't you?"

"There will be a slight delay until a table is ready," the moose would say, and snort, and shake himself.

Mr. Breton was very happy in the kitchen. There were pots of all sorts of good things steaming on the stove and smelling good, and bread baking in the oven from morning to night. Mr. Breton loved to cook good things for lots of people, the more the better. He had never been so busy and happy in his life.

One morning, Mr. Bobowicz, the game warden, came to the restaurant. "Mr. Breton, are you aware of Section 5—Subheading 6—Paragraph 3 of the state fish and game laws?" said Mr. Bobowicz.

"No, I am not aware of Section 5—Subheading 6—Paragraph 3," Mr. Breton said. "What is it all about?"

"No person shall keep a moose as a pet, tie up a moose, keep a moose in a pen or barn, or parlor or bedroom, or any such enclosure," said Mr. Bobowicz. "In short, it is against the law to have a tame moose."

"Oh my," said Mr. Breton, "I don't want to do anything against the law. But I don't keep the moose. He just came along one day, and has stayed ever since. He helps me run my restaurant."

Mr. Bobowicz rubbed his chin. "And where is the aforesaid moose?"

Mr. Breton had given the moose one of the rooms upstairs, in which there was a particularly large bed. The moose just fit in the bed, if he folded up his feet. He liked it very much; he said he never had a bed of his own. The moose slept on the bed under six blankets, and during the day he would go upstairs sometimes, and stretch out on the bed and sigh with pleasure.

When Mr. Bobowicz came to see Mr. Breton, the moose had been downstairs to help Mr. Breton eat a giant breakfast, and then he had wandered back to his room to enjoy lying on his bed until the lunchtime customers arrived. He heard Mr. Breton and Mr. Bobowicz talking. The moose bugled. He had never bugled in Mr. Breton's house before. Bugling is a noise that no animal except a moose can really do right. Elk can bugle, and elephants can bugle, and some kinds of geese and swans can bugle, but it is nothing like moose bugling. When the moose bugled, the whole house jumped and rattled, dishes clinked together in the cupboard, pots and pans clanged together, icicles fell off the house.

"I AM NOT A TAME MOOSE!" the moose shouted from where he was lying on his bed.

Mr. Bobowicz looked at Mr. Breton with very wide eyes. "Was that the moose?"

The moose had gotten out of bed, and was clumping down the stairs. "You're flipping right, that was the moose," he growled.

The moose clumped right up to Mr. Bobowicz, and looked at him with one red eye. The moose's nose was touching Mr. Bobowicz's nose. They just stood there, looking at each other, for a long time. The moose was breathing loudly, and his eye seemed to be a glowing

coal. Mr. Bobowicz's knees were shaking. Then the moose spoke very slowly. "You . . . are . . . a . . . tame . . . game warden."

The moose turned, and clumped back up the stairs. Mr. Breton and Mr. Bobowicz heard him sigh and heard the springs crash and groan as he flopped onto the big bed.

"Mr. Bobowicz, the moose is not tame," Mr. Breton said. "He is a wild moose, and he lives here of his own free will; he is the headwaiter." Mr. Breton spoke very quietly, because Mr. Bobowicz had not moved since the moose had come downstairs. His eyes were still open very wide, and his knees were still shaking. Mr. Breton took Mr. Bobowicz by the hand, and led him into the kitchen and poured him a cup of coffee.

Dave

• • • • • •

NOT VERY FAR from Mr. Breton's house, in a secret place in the woods, lived a hermit named Dave. Everybody knew that Dave was out there, but nobody ever saw him. Mr. Bobowicz, the game warden, had seen what might have been Dave a couple of times; or it might have been a shadow. Sometimes, late at night, Mr. Breton would hear the wind whistling strangely, and think of Dave.

The moose brought Dave home with him one night. They were old friends. Dave was dressed in rabbit skins, stitched together. His feet were wrapped in tree bark and moose-moss. An owl sat on his head.

"Dave is very shy," the moose said. "He would ap-

preciate it if you didn't say anything to him until he knows you better, maybe in ten or fifteen years. He knows about your gingerbread, and he would like to try it." While the moose spoke, Dave blushed very red, and tried to cover his face with the owl, which fluttered and squawked.

Mr. Breton put dishes with gingerbread and applesauce and fresh whipped cream in front of Dave, the moose, and the owl. There was no noise but the moose slurping, and Dave's spoon scraping. Mr. Breton turned to get the coffeepot. When he looked back at the table, Dave and the owl were gone.

"Dave says thank you," the moose said.

The next night Dave was back, and this time he had a whistle made out of a turkey bone in his hat. After the gingerbread, Dave played on the whistle, like the wind making strange sounds, the moose hummed, and Mr. Breton clicked two spoons, while the owl hopped up and down on the kitchen table, far into the night.

Hums of a moose

● ● ● ● ● ● ● ● ● ● ● ● ● ● ● ● ●

ONE DAY, after the moose had been staying with Mr.
Breton for a fairly long time, there was an especially
heavy snowfall. The snow got to be as high as the house,
and there was no way for people to come from the town.

Mr. Breton got a big fire going in the stove, and kept
adding pieces of wood until the stove was glowing red.
The house was warm, and filled with the smell of applesauce, which Mr. Breton was cooking in big pots on the
stove. Mr. Breton was peeling apples and the moose was
sitting on the floor, lapping every now and then at a big
chowder bowl full of coffee on the kitchen table.

The moose didn't say anything. Mr. Breton didn't say anything. Now and then the moose would take a deep breath with his nose in the air, sniffing in the smell of apples and cinnamon and raisins cooking. Then he would sigh. The sighs got louder and longer.

The moose began to hum—softly, then louder. The humming made the table shake, and Mr. Breton felt the humming in his fingers each time he picked up an apple. The humming mixed with the apple and cinnamon smell and melted the frost on the windows, and the room filled with sunlight. Mr. Breton smelled flowers.

Then he could see them. The kitchen floor had turned into a meadow with new grass, dandelions, periwinkles, and daisies.

The moose hummed. Mr. Breton smelled melting snow. He heard ice cracking. He felt the ground shake under the hoofs of moose returning from the low, wet places. Rabbits bounded through the fields. Bears, thin after the winter's sleep, came out of hiding. Birds sang.

The people in the town could not remember such an unseasonable thaw. The weather got warm all of a sudden,

and the ice and snow melted for four days before winter set in again. When they went to Mr. Breton's restaurant, they discovered that he had made a wonderful stew with lots of carrots that reminded them of meadows in springtime.

Moose moving
· · · · · · · · · · · · · · · · · ·

WHEN SPRING finally came, the moose became moody. He spent a lot of time staring out the back door. Flocks of geese flew overhead, returning to lakes in the North, and the moose always stirred when he heard their honking.

"Chef," the moose said one morning, "I will be going tomorrow. I wonder if you would pack some gingerbread for me to take along."

Mr. Breton baked a special batch of gingerbread, and packed it in parcels tied with string, so the moose could hang them from his antlers. When the moose came downstairs, Mr. Breton was sitting in the kitchen drinking coffee. The parcels of gingerbread were on the kitchen table.

"Do you want a bowl of coffee before you go?" Mr. Breton asked.

"Thank you," said the moose.

"I shall certainly miss you," Mr. Breton said.

"Thank you," said the moose.

"You are the best friend I have," said Mr. Breton.

"Thank you," said the moose.

"Do you suppose you'll ever come back?" Mr. Breton asked.

"Not before Thursday or Friday," said the moose. "It would be impolite to visit my uncle for less than a week."

The moose hooked his antlers into the loops of string on the packages of gingerbread. "My uncle will like this." He stood up and turned to the door.

"Wait!" Mr. Breton shouted. "Do you mean that you are not leaving forever? I thought you were lonely for the life of a wild moose. I thought you wanted to go back to the wild, free places."

"Chef, do you have any idea of how cold it gets in the

wild, free places?" the moose said. "And the food! Terrible!"

"Have a nice time at your uncle's," said Mr. Breton.

"I'll send you a postcard," said the moose.

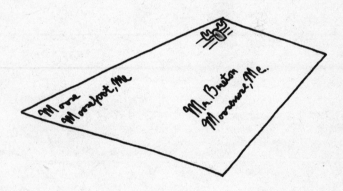

Return of
the Moose

for Bill Watson

1
...

FOR A LONG time, the blue moose had been helping Mr. Breton run his restaurant on the edge of the big woods. The moose had turned up one winter day, and gone to work as the headwaiter. Actually, he was the only waiter. Mr. Breton did the cooking, and the moose took care of the customers. Mr. Breton liked the arrangement. He had been lonely before the blue moose came, and the customers were much more polite to the moose than they had been to Mr. Breton. It's not easy to be impolite to an animal over eight feet tall.

Mr. Breton and the moose were friends, but they didn't talk very much. The moose did his work, Mr.

Breton did his work, and the people who came to eat in the restaurant were satisfied. Late in the evening, when all the cleaning up had been done, Mr. Breton and the moose would sit together, and drink coffee. Mr. Breton drank his coffee from a cup. The blue moose drank coffee from a soup bowl. Sometimes the moose would help Mr. Breton in the kitchen, and they would sing together. The moose didn't sing so much as hum. He had a very nice humming voice.

On Sundays, and between mealtimes, when there was no one in the restaurant, the blue moose would go for long walks in the woods and meadows, or sit in his room upstairs. Sometimes, the moose would take a vacation, and go off to visit moose friends or relatives.

The moose never talked about his life before he came to the restaurant, and Mr. Breton was too polite to ask questions. Mr. Breton never talked about his life before he opened the restaurant, because opening the restaurant was the second most interesting thing that ever happened to him. The first most interesting thing that ever happened to Mr. Breton was when the blue moose came to help him.

Sometimes friends dropped by. Mr. Bobowicz, the game warden, would come to visit, and Dave, a hermit who lived in the woods, liked to come late at night with his pet owl. When friends came, they would sit in the kitchen with Mr. Breton and the blue moose, and drink coffee, and eat hot gingerbread. Sometimes they would sing.

When Mr. Breton and the moose talked, they would usually discuss business matters having to do with the restaurant.

"Chef," the moose would say, "when I go into town tomorrow for supplies, do you want me to get some parsnips? We're almost out of parsnips."

"Yes," Mr. Breton would say, "and if you can find some very nice turnips, get those too. I'm thinking about experimenting with turnips in my beef stew."

"That's a very good idea, Chef," the moose would say.

"Thank you," Mr. Breton would say. "I spent all day Wednesday thinking about it."

"It is an inspiration, Chef," the moose would say.

"Thank you very much," Mr. Breton would say.

One day, the moose said to Mr. Breton, "Chef, in the basement of this restaurant, I noticed an old typewriter. Would it be all right if I kept that in my room?"

"Of course," Mr. Breton said. Then he said, "I hope you don't mind my asking. I hope you don't think I'm impolite. But what does a moose want with a typewriter?"

"I'm going to type with it, Chef," said the moose.

"Oh," said Mr. Breton.

2
...

THE NEXT morning, when Mr. Breton was preparing
things in the kitchen, at the time when the moose
usually stayed in bed, Mr. Breton heard the clicking
of a typewriter from the moose's room. The moose
typed slowly, one click at a time. He kept it up for
more than an hour.

At the time when the moose usually came downstairs for his soup bowl of coffee and fifteen or twenty
pieces of gingerbread, he was still clicking away on the
typewriter. Mr. Breton put the soup bowl of coffee
and fifteen or twenty pieces of gingerbread on a tray

and carried it upstairs. He knocked softly on the door of the moose's room.

"Come in," said the blue moose.

Mr. Breton went in. The moose was sitting in bed with the typewriter balanced on his knees. Surrounding him were stacks of paper with writing in longhoof. There was also a pile of neatly typed pages. The moose was reading from the sheets of paper written in longhoof, and typing what he read.

"I hope my typing does not disturb you," said the moose. "If it bothers you while you are cooking, I could type at another time."

"No, no, not at all," Mr. Breton said. "I like the sound of the typing. It reminds me of drops of rain falling on the roof. I just thought you might like it if I brought your coffee and gingerbread to you."

"Thank you," said the moose. "That was most considerate."

"I don't suppose you'd want to tell me what you are writing," Mr. Breton said.

"Not at this time," said the moose.

From that time on, every morning, the moose typed

in his room while Mr. Breton worked in the kitchen. Every morning, Mr. Breton brought a soup bowl of coffee and fifteen or twenty pieces of gingerbread to the moose. Every morning, Mr. Breton said, "How is it going today?"

"Just fine," the moose would say.

"I don't suppose you'd want to tell me what you are writing," Mr. Breton would say.

"Not at this time," the moose would say.

Mr. Breton would go back to the kitchen. For a while there would be no sound of typing, as the moose slurped up his soup bowl of coffee, and ate his fifteen or twenty pieces of gingerbread. Then the clicking would start again, reminding Mr. Breton of drops of rain falling on the roof.

Mr. Breton was very curious about what the blue moose was writing, but whenever he asked the moose, the moose would say, "Not at this time."

3
...

ONE MORNING when Mr. Breton came down to begin
work in the kitchen, he found the blue moose standing
and staring out of the kitchen window.

"You're up early," Mr. Breton said.

The moose said nothing.

"No typing this morning?" Mr. Breton said.

The moose said nothing.

"Coffee?" Mr. Breton said.

The moose said nothing.

"You're not mad at me, are you?" Mr. Breton said.

The moose said nothing.

Mr. Breton set about making a big pot of coffee.

When it was ready, he said, "Moose, come and have some coffee."

The moose sighed. When a moose sighs, it is always very expressive. This sigh was even more expressive than usual. It made the dishes in the cupboards rattle and clatter. It made the windows and the stovepipe rattle and buzz. It made two flies, who had been circling near the ceiling, stop, listen, forget to move their wings, and fall to the floor. It made little ripples in the coffee in Mr. Breton's cup, and in the soup bowl he had filled for the moose.

"Something bothering you?" Mr. Breton asked.

The moose sighed again. The dishes rattled, the windows and stovepipe buzzed. The two flies looked at each other, and began crawling toward the kitchen door. Little waves appeared on the surface of the coffee.

"Oh, an artist's life is hard, Chef—hard, hard, hard," the blue moose said.

"Yes, I suppose it is," Mr. Breton said. "Is that why you were sighing?"

"My work, my life, my masterpiece!" the moose

said. "Everything has gone sour! It seemed to be going so well, and now . . . disaster!"

"Does this have something to do with all the typing you've been doing?" Mr. Breton asked.

"Oh, why, *why*, WHY am I punished like this?" the moose moaned. Then he clumped upstairs. Mr. Breton heard the bedsprings crash and groan, as the moose hurled himself into bed.

That day the moose did not come downstairs to help Mr. Breton. Mr. Breton had to do all the cooking, and wait on the customers. The moose stayed in his bed all day, with a newspaper over his head.

Every now and then, when things weren't too busy in the restaurant, Mr. Breton would go upstairs and peek into the moose's room. The blue moose sat in his bed, with the newspaper covering his head, and said nothing.

After the last customer had gone, Mr. Breton brought the moose a big bowl of beef stew with turnips.

"Leave it on the table," the moose said.

The moose stayed in bed, with the newspaper over

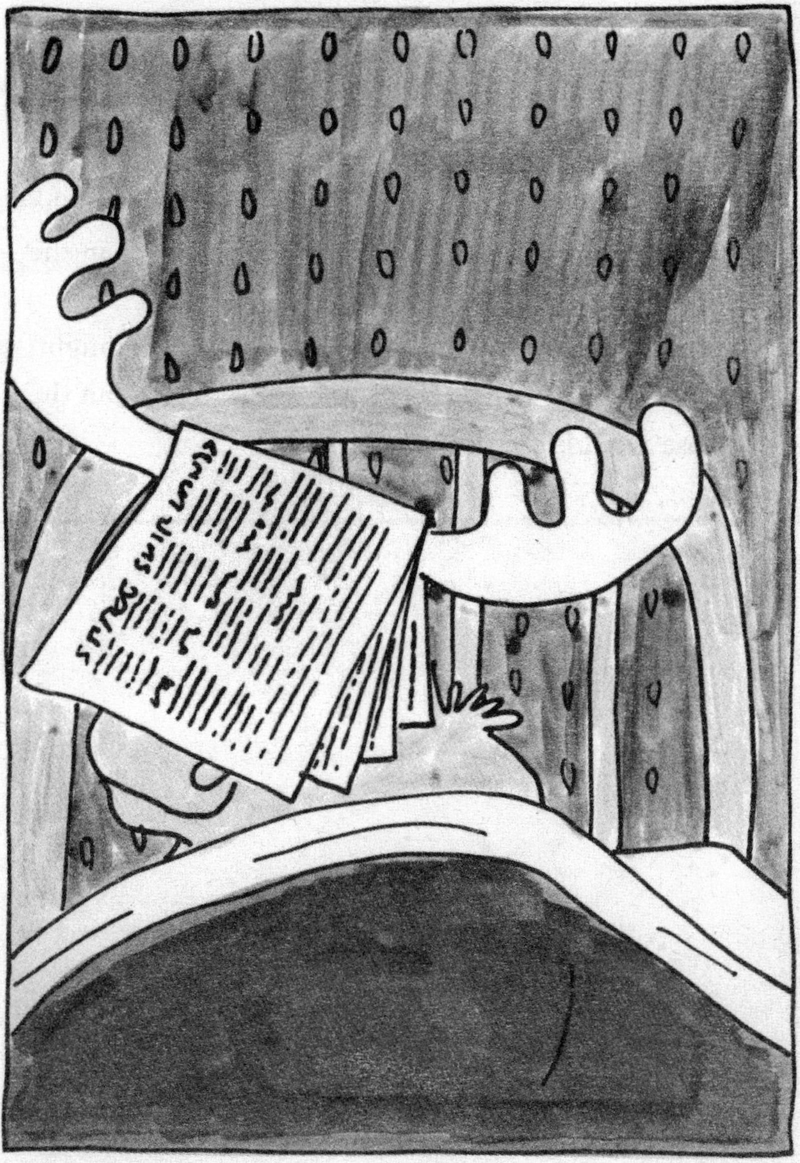

his head for five days. Mr. Bobowicz, the game warden, and Dave, the hermit, came to visit the moose, but he wouldn't talk to them. He just sat in bed, with a newspaper covering his head. Every now and then the moose would sigh, and frighten the customers in the restaurant.

Mr. Breton was worried about the moose. At night, he would sit in a chair beside the moose's bed, but the moose wouldn't talk to him.

4
...

ON THE SIXTH day, when Mr. Breton went down to the kitchen to begin his work, he heard the moose typing in his room. Mr. Breton smiled. He made a big pot of coffee, and a fresh batch of gingerbread. When the gingerbread was ready, he poured applesauce all over it. The moose liked it that way. He put twenty-five pieces of gingerbread on a tray, and went up to the moose's room.

"Good morning, Chef," the moose said. "It's a beautiful morning, isn't it? I see you've brought me some gingerbread. How thoughtful! Thank you, Chef, ever so much."

"I guess things are going better with whatever it is you've been writing," Mr. Breton said.

"My book?" said the moose. "My masterpiece? My work of literature? It couldn't be better. I'll have it finished this afternoon."

"Oh, it's a book you've been writing," Mr. Breton said.

"Not just a book," said the blue moose. "Not just any book—it is a great book, the most wonderful book ever written by man or moose. I'll admit I had a bit of trouble with it for a while, but that's all behind me now. This will be the greatest book anybody has ever seen . . . the greatest book ever written—and, Chef, I wonder if you'd do me a favor . . ."

"Of course," said Mr. Breton.

"I'd like you to be the first person to read my book," the blue moose said.

"It would be an honor," said Mr. Breton.

"Tonight after the restaurant closes," said the moose.

That night, after Mr. Breton had finished his work, the moose went upstairs to get his book. Mr. Breton cleared the big table in the kitchen, and poured a cup of coffee for himself, and a soup bowl of coffee for the moose. Mr. Breton put on his reading glasses, took them off, cleaned them with the tail of his shirt, put them on again, took them off again, cleaned them some more, put them on again, and sat down to wait for the moose.

The moose brought down the book he had written and put it on the kitchen table in front of Mr. Breton. He had also drawn some pictures to go with the book, and they were tucked in, here and there, between the typed pages.

Mr. Breton began to read. The moose paced up and down in the kitchen. "How do you like it so far?" the moose asked him.

"I've just begun to read the first sentence," Mr. Breton said.

Mr. Breton continued to read. "Oh, my!" he said.

"What? What?" the moose said. "What part are you reading now?"

"I was just going to say . . ." Mr. Breton said. "Oh, my! I can't read with you pacing up and down like

that. Now sit down and drink your coffee while I read your book."

The moose sat down. Mr. Breton read. This is the book that Mr. Breton read. This is the book the moose had written, the book that Mr. Breton read at the kitchen table, in the evening, after the restaurant had closed.

5
···

THE TRUE STORY OF A WILD MOOSE
by D. Moosus Moosewater

After single-handedly defeating Nazi Germany and
Imperial Japan, and thus ending World War II, I decided to devote myself to finding a cure for all diseases
known to Man and Moose. However, before I was able
to do this, I found that my country still needed me to
serve as President of the United States. In those days,
I was known by the name of Harry S. Truman.

While being President was a great honor, I found
the job boring. The only parts I liked were my vaca-

tions. During one vacation, I set the world's record for holding my breath under water—two hours and forty-three minutes. I also set the still-unbroken world's records for the high jump, the hundred-yard dash, and the mile. Due to a technicality, my records were not official. It turned out that four-footed creatures are not allowed to compete, so my name is not in the record books. I was disappointed, and I gave up sports.

On another vacation, I discovered the largest gold mine on earth, under a vacant lot in Bayonne, New Jersey, and gave it as a present to the United States. But my favorite vacation was the one during which I became the first moose to climb Mount Everest. I climbed it three times. I could have climbed it more, but on the third day of my vacation, I received an urgent message to come back to the White House.

After I got through being President of the United States, I decided to devote some time to space travel, so I designed and built all the rockets and space vehicles which would be used later to carry men to the Moon. I had already had a lot of experience inventing things. I had already invented the jet airplane, color

television, computers, and the cheeseburger.

Of all my great adventures, the most exciting, and the one that presented the greatest danger to Earth, was the invasion of the Moose from Space. At the time this happened, I was busy carving the heads of Washington, Jefferson, Lincoln, and Teddy Roosevelt on Mount Rushmore. A message was brought to me that a spaceship had landed in Washington, D.C., not far from the Capitol. Out of the spaceship had come a gigantic moose, more than fifty feet high. The moose refused to move. He just stood there, demanding that the President of the United States, and all the presidents and kings on Earth, assemble outside his spaceship no later than the following Tuesday.

Fearing that the Moose from Space had hostile intentions, the army and police had shot him, bombed him, set fire to him, set dynamite off under him, set vicious dogs after him, squirted him with insect spray, and thrown big rocks at him. None of this had the slightest effect on the Moose from Space. He did seem less friendly after all these attempts to subdue him, but he still refused to move.

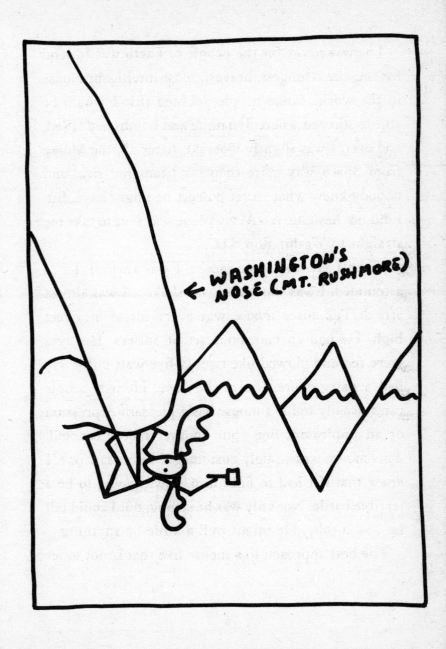

← WASHINGTON'S NOSE (MT. RUSHMORE)

The last resort for the people of Earth was to send for me, the strongest, bravest, most intelligent moose in the world. Some people doubted that I would be able to succeed where dynamite and bombs had failed, and even I was slightly worried. After all, the Moose from Space was more than six times my size, and nobody knew what secret powers he might have. But I did not hesitate. An Army plane was sent to take me straight to Washington, D.C.

When I saw the space moose, I was amazed. I was astounded. I was shocked. I was shaken. I was almost afraid. The space moose was every bit of fifty feet high. He had an enormous set of antlers. His eyes were red and glowed like twenty-five-watt bulbs. He had a nasty expression on his face. Human people can't usually tell if a moose has a pleasant expression or an unpleasant one—but another moose can tell. This moose was an ugly customer if I ever saw one. I knew that if I had to fight him, it was going to be a terrible battle. Not only was he strong, but I could tell he was sneaky. He might pull a knife or anything.

The best approach to a moose like that is not to let

him know that you are afraid. I marched right up to him. "What do you want here, you big palooka?" I asked him.

The space moose sneered an ugly sneer. "Go away, sonny, you bother me," he said.

He was trying to get me mad. I knew that if I made a rash move, the space moose would thump me with his antlers, which probably weighed a ton. I remained cool. "Where I come from," I said, "the people eat moose of your size in sandwiches, horns and all. Now tell me what you want before I get ugly."

No moose on Earth likes to have his antlers referred to as "horns," and apparently space moose are just the same. The big moose began to breathe hard through his nose. "If you're a moose," he said, "and not a mouse—which you might be, judging from your size —you should know better than to talk that way."

"I'm a moose all right," I said, "and what are you? You look like a great big dairy cow to me."

"You're about to get into trouble, peewee," the space moose said.

The space moose was getting really mad now. That

was what I wanted. If I had to fight him, I wanted him to make some foolish moves. "I'm tired of all this social chatter," I said. "Now tell me what you're doing here before I call the farmer who takes care of you."

That did it. The space moose was in a perfect rage. "I'll tell you," he snorted, "before I trample you into a moose-flavored pizza, I'll tell you exactly what I'm doing here." The space moose was so angry now that he couldn't stand still. He was so angry that his ears were actually spinning like the propellers on an airplane. "What I'm doing here, you miserable pipsqueak," the space moose said, "what I'm doing here is waiting for the people of Earth to surrender no later than next Tuesday. I come from a planet in the galaxy of Betelmoose, where all the inhabitants are big, tough moose like me. Every now and then, we take over a planet, and push everybody around, and destroy things just for fun. I'm the biggest, toughest moose, so they send me down first to make everybody surrender. Then, I call the other moose on the radio, and they all come down here, and we have a good time. And we don't leave until the place is a real mess. But right now, I'm going to make mooseburger out of you."

"Wait a minute while I tie one hoof behind my back," I said.

The space moose made a dive for me with his antlers. I made a deft move to the side, and he missed me. Then he reared up and tried to get me with his hooves. I dodged out of the way, and bit him on the rump for good measure. That made him even madder, and he began striking out in every direction. His punches were wild. He never touched me. Every now and then, I'd see a chance, and poke him—with my hoof, with my antlers—thrust and parry—turn and thrust —butt and kick. The space moose was confused. He didn't know where he was. I was in complete control of the fight—but the space moose never got tired. One-sixth his size, I had to do a lot of moving to keep out of the way of his punishing hooves and antlers. I saw that I'd have to find some way to finish the fight before I started to get tired myself. In the course of our battle, we had covered a lot of distance. I realized that we had fought our way over to the Washington Monument. I managed to move around so that the Washington

Monument was behind me. Then I pretended to be tired. I stopped moving and just stood there, pretending to be trying to get my breath. The space moose stopped too. This was what he was waiting for. He was slower but stronger. He knew that when I got tired, I would be at his mercy.

The space moose took a couple of steps backward. He was getting ready to charge. I pretended to be too tired to move out of the way. Then he put his head down, and ran at me. At the last moment, I jumped about fifteen feet to one side. His antlers were so wide that he just missed me by inches as he crashed directly into the base of the Washington Monument. He staggered backward, still on his feet. The force of the impact broke off the top sixty or seventy feet of the monument, which fell in one piece, and bounced off his head. He sat down, dazed.

The space moose shook his head. "How did you do that?" he asked.

"Never mind, bozo," I said. "Just get into your little airplane and fly off before I lose my temper."

The space moose staggered off and got into his

spaceship, and lifted off. I received a platinum medal, and a check for fifty billion dollars from a grateful Earth. The Washington Monument was repaired, of course. I did it free of charge.

And that is how I saved Earth from the space moose invaders and had my greatest adventure.

The End

"Well," said the blue moose, "how did you like it?"

"It's very exciting," Mr. Breton said. "Is any of it true?"

"Humph!" snorted the moose, and gathered up his pages and pictures, and went upstairs.

6
...

The next morning, the blue moose went into town with a big, flat package, wrapped in brown paper and tied with string. It was his book. He told Mr. Breton that he was mailing it to a publishing house, Klotz, Yold & Company, Inc.

"Do you think they'll publish it?" Mr. Breton asked.

"Chef, you amaze me," the moose said. "You read it, didn't you? It is a masterpiece. Not only will Klotz, Yold & Company, Inc. publish it, but it will make me rich and famous."

"Do you really think so?" Mr. Breton asked.

"Chef, you know a great deal about cooking," said

the moose, "but apparently you know absolutely nothing about literature. Do I really think so? What a question! Klotz, Yold & Company, Inc. will shed tears of joy when they read my book. You'll see."

Then the moose sat down at the kitchen table, and looked out the window with a dreamy expression. Mr. Breton could tell that the moose was thinking about the days to come, when Klotz, Yold & Company, Inc. would publish his book, and he would become rich and famous.

For several weeks, the moose was very little help around the restaurant. He seemed to be unable to pay attention to his work. He would bring customers things they had not ordered, and not bring them things they had ordered. He would bring them their dessert at the beginning of the meal, and he would bring them their soup at the end of the meal. Several times, when the customers handed their menus to the moose, after looking at them, the moose would sign his autograph on the menus, and hand them back to the customers.

None of the customers complained about the

moose's strange behavior. After all, who wants to argue with a moose? But Mr. Breton noticed it. He knew what was causing it. He knew that the moose was waiting to hear from Klotz, Yold & Company, Inc. Weeks went by.

The blue moose never gave up expecting that Klotz, Yold & Company, Inc. would want to publish his book. Once, Mr. Breton tried to bring up the subject. He tried to suggest the possibility that Klotz, Yold & Company, Inc. might, for whatever reasons, not want to publish the moose's book. "Nonsense," the moose said.

Mr. Breton was starting to worry about the moose. He was worried that Klotz, Yold & Company, Inc. might turn the book down, and make the moose very unhappy. In fact, he thought that Klotz, Yold & Company, Inc. *would* turn the book down. Mr. Breton thought it wasn't a very good book.

He talked to Mr. Bobowicz, the game warden about it. "The moose has written a book," Mr. Breton said. "It is all about how he won World War II, and was President of the United States, and climbed Mount

Everest, and found a gold mine, and invented color television, and the cheeseburger. He says, in his book, that he fought a fifty-foot-tall moose from outer space. There isn't a single word of truth in it. Now he's sent it off to a publisher, and he's sure they will want to publish it, and make him rich and famous. Of course, the publisher will know that the book isn't true, and refuse to publish it. The moose will be so disappointed. I'm worried about him."

The next day, the moose received a letter from Klotz, Yold & Company, Inc., saying that they wanted to publish his book, and would he come to New York and talk with them about it.

7
• • •

Mr. Breton and Mr. Bobowicz, the game warden, saw the blue moose off at the train. Dave, the hermit, didn't actually come to the train, but they knew he was hiding in the trees at the edge of the tracks. Mr. Breton had packed sandwiches and a lot of ginger-bread for the moose to eat on the trip. They all waved good-bye until the train was out of sight.

"I knew it!" Mr. Breton said to Mr. Bobowicz. "I knew the blue moose was going to be famous!"

The following day, the moose came back. He had presents for everybody. He gave Mr. Breton a real French chef's spoon. He gave Mr. Bobowicz a whistle

with a compass built in. He gave Dave a little note-
book covered in red leather (Dave liked to make up
poems), and a pencil that wrote in different colors.

For himself, the moose had bought a pair of eyeglasses, without any glass in them, and a pipe. He also
gave Mr. Breton, Mr. Bobowicz, and Dave copies of a
photograph of himself, wearing his eyeglasses and
smoking his pipe. Klotz, Yold & Company, Inc., the
publishers, had taken the picture to print on the back
of the moose's book.

Mr. Breton was very proud of the moose. "How did
it go?" he asked the moose.

"I signed a contract," the moose said. "They're
going to print my book. They say that they may have
to edit it a little—sort of fix up little parts, here and
there—but they like it very much."

A long time passed. Mr. Breton could hardly wait
for the moose's book to be published. The moose
couldn't wait at all. He went out to look for the mail
every five or ten minutes. In between, he practiced
signing his autograph. The moose spent a lot of time
looking at the photograph of himself wearing his eye-

glasses and smoking his pipe.

One day a package arrived. It was from Klotz, Yold & Company, Inc. The moose was so excited that he couldn't unwrap it. Mr. Breton had to help him. "It's my book! It's my book!" the moose kept repeating. "It's *The True Story of a Wild Moose!*"

Mr. Breton unwrapped the book. On the cover was a picture of a lady moose wearing lipstick and long eyelashes. Over the picture of the lady moose was printing: "Hot Mooselove!" it said. There was more printing—

She was a sweet unspoiled moosegirl
until she met
THE MOOSE FROM SPACE
An exciting love story!!!

Nowhere on the cover of the book did it say *The True Story of a Wild Moose.* For a moment, Mr. Breton and the moose thought that maybe it wasn't the blue moose's book. They thought that maybe it was some other book—but there on the back of the book was the

picture of the moose wearing his eyeglasses and smoking his pipe.

The moose roared. It was a terrible roar. It broke fifteen plates, two windows, and a cast-iron frying pan. "This is not my book!" the moose shouted. "There is no moosegirl in my book! There is no love story in my book! They changed everything! They said they were going to fix it up here and there—and they've changed everything!" Then the blue moose roared again, causing the paint to peel off the ceiling, and curdling twenty-six quarts of milk in the icebox —and rushed out of the kitchen, out of the restaurant, and out of sight.

8
...

THE BLUE MOOSE went missing. He was gone for two days. Mr. Breton closed the restaurant. He and Mr. Bobowicz, the game warden, and Dave, the hermit, spent all day looking for the moose. At night, they went out with flashlights. Mr. Bobowicz kept blowing the whistle the moose had given him. They didn't find him.

At last, the three men came back to the restaurant. They sat in the kitchen. Every so often, one of them would say, "Where can he be?"

The moose walked in. "Chef, can you fix me something for an upset stomach?" he said. "I've eaten six thousand copies of *The Moose from Space* and two electric typewriters, and I'm feeling just a little bit ill."

Mr. Breton, Mr. Bobowicz, the game warden, and Dave, the hermit, all jumped up and began talking at once.

"Where have you been?"

"Why did you run off like that?"

"We were all worried!"

Mr. Breton prepared a glass of fizzy stuff for the moose's upset stomach, and the blue moose drank it. "Another," he said.

"Moose," Mr. Breton said, as he prepared another glass of fizzy stuff, "please tell us where you've been."

"I've been to New York City," the moose said, "I've been to the book warehouse of Klotz, Yold & Company, Inc. That's where I ate all six thousand copies of that monstrosity they made out of my book. Then I went to the offices of Klotz, Yold & Company, Inc. and had a little talk with the people there. I explained to them that I wanted them to print my book, just the way it was written. That's where I ate the two electric typewriters. It wasn't that I was hungry—I just wanted to demonstrate to them that I am a very serious moose. They saw it my way, and they are going to print *The True Story of a Wild Moose*, just the way I wrote it."

"My goodness," Mr. Breton said.

"Yes, well, business can be very tiring," said the blue moose. "If you'll all excuse me, I think I'll go to bed now."

9
...

A week later, Klotz, Yold & Company, Inc. sent the blue moose a copy of his book. On the cover was a picture of the fight between the moose and the space moose. "That's better," said the blue moose.

The book was a big success. Soon, the moose began getting letters every day. People asked him to come to schools and libraries and talk to audiences. Newspapers and magazines printed stories about the moose. The moose started to appear on television.

Mr. Breton bought a television set so he could watch the moose. Mr. Bobowicz, the game warden, and Dave, the hermit, would come to Mr. Breton's restau-

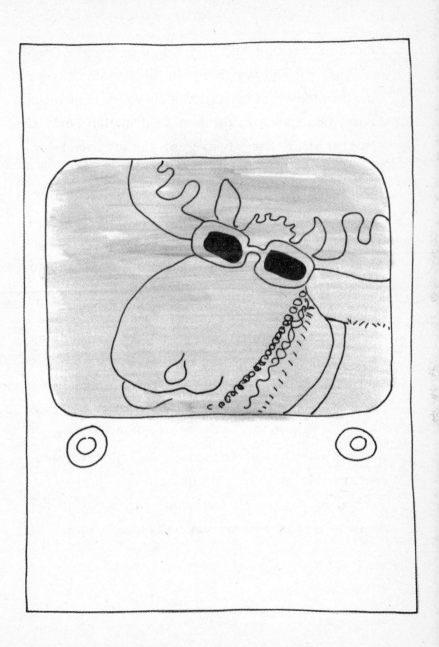

rant in the evening, and they would sit together, eating popcorn, and watching the blue moose. Every time the moose was interviewed, he would remember to say, "By the way, the best food in the world is served at Mr. Breton's restaurant, and my friend, Mr. Breton, is the best chef in the world."

Although he appreciated the compliment, Mr. Breton wished the moose wouldn't say that. It was hard for him to take care of all the people who had come to eat in his restaurant, since the moose had become famous—especially without the moose there to help him.

The moose was away, giving interviews, and talking to people more than he was at home. Mr. Breton was happy for his friend. He was glad that his book was a big success, and that he was famous—but he missed the days when the moose was always there. He missed the days when he and the moose would run the restaurant together, quietly, not talking much.

Then Klotz, Yold & Company, Inc. wrote to the moose to say that a movie was going to be made of *The*

True Story of a Wild Moose, and that he, the moose, was wanted in Hollywood.

Mr. Breton gave a good-bye party for the blue moose. He made a special carrot cake. Mr. Bobowicz, the game warden, was there, and Dave, the hermit. The moose's friends tried to make it a happy party, but they were all sad to think that their friend was going so far away.

The moose went to Hollywood. He sent picture postcards to Mr. Breton. Once, Mr. Breton saw the moose on a television show from Hollywood. The blue moose had a lot of little gold ornaments on chains around his neck. He was wearing sunglasses, and a pink sweater.

The movie came out. Mr. Breton, Mr. Bobowicz, the game warden, and Dave, the hermit, went to see it. Dave was worried about going into the theater with so many people, because he was so shy. Mr. Breton and Mr. Bobowicz finally solved the problem by giving Dave a paper bag, with eye holes cut out, to wear over his head. It was a good movie. The movie people

had made a very realistic space moose. Robert Blueford, a famous actor, played the part of the blue moose.

Even though it was a good movie, Mr. Breton was sad when he got home. He thought that the moose would probably stay in Hollywood, writing books and movies. He thought he should probably find someone to help him in the restaurant—but he really didn't want to.

10
· · ·

THE NEXT MORNING, the morning after Mr. Breton had
gone to see the movie of *The True Story of a Wild Moose*,
he found the blue moose in the kitchen.

"Chef," said the moose, "we appear to be very low
on onions, butter, carrots, and flour. Is there anything
else I should get?"

"Moose! You came back!" Mr. Breton shouted.

"Naturally," said the moose. "Did I ever say I
wouldn't?"

"No, you didn't," Mr. Breton said, "but I thought
you were going to live in Hollywood and be a famous
writer."

"Well, I did consider it," the moose said, "but it got to be very boring. Besides, they had that fellow, Robert Blueford, play me in the movie, and they could have had me. Chef, there are very few people with really good taste in this country. That's why I'd rather stay here with you."

"Are you going to write any more books?" Mr. Breton asked.

"I don't think so," the moose said. "I thought I'd get to work on finding a cure for every disease known to Man or Moose."

"That's a very good idea," Mr. Breton said.

"It may take quite a while," said the blue moose. "I hope you don't mind if I continue to work around the restaurant while I do my research."

"Not at all," Mr. Breton said.

"Thanks, Chef," the moose said. "I'll go and get the groceries now."

The Author